To Hara, Jordyn, Saul, and anyone who gets worried—HA

To my family—SP

Library of Congress Cataloging-in-Publication data is on file with the publisher.

Text copyright © 2020 by Hallee Adelman
Illustrations copyright © 2020 by Albert Whitman & Company
Illustrations by Sandra de la Prada
First published in the United States of America in 2020 by Albert Whitman & Company
ISBN 978-0-8075-8686-0 (hardcover)
ISBN 978-0-8075-8680-8 (ebook)

Printed in China
10 9 8 7 6 5 4 3 2 1 WKT 24 23 22 21 20

Design by Nina Simoneaux

For more information about Albert Whitman & Company,
visit our website at www.albertwhitman.com.

My brother Bax wasn't going to Juan's superhero birthday party with me.
I felt a little worried.
How could I go without my sidekick?

Dad said, "You'll be okay. Take three very deep breaths, and go get dressed."

I tugged on my favorite costume.
It looked too small.
Would everyone laugh?
Now I was really worried.

I headed toward Juan's.
I was late.
Who else would be there?
Would Juan hang out with me?
Would I feel left out?

I felt way past worried
with my heart thumping
and my mind racing
and my worry growing.

RUFF! RUFF!
Pickles knocked me down with his muddy paws.
Now my costume looked even worse.

TLING! TLING!
Keya and Hooper scootered right past me.
Why didn't they stop?
"It's party time!" they cheered.

What if it was the worst party ever...
I'd walk in late, and no one would talk to me.

Or else someone would talk to me, but I wouldn't know what to say.

Or else everyone would laugh at my costume.
HA! HA! HA!

When I got to the gate, I saw everyone's costumes looked better than mine.
They were already playing without me.

I didn't feel like a superhero.
I wanted to go home.
But just like Dad said, I took
three very deep breaths.

My heart pounded
thump, thump,
thump, thump,
thump, thump,
but I inched forward.

Until...
HA! HA! HA!
HA! HA! HA!
Everyone was laughing.
I knew they weren't
laughing at me,
but it felt like they were.

I ran off. I didn't know what else to do.
I heard Juan ask, "Where's Brock?"
I wanted to call out, "I'm right here, Juan."

But my worry was in the way,
and my words wouldn't come out.

I heard a sound up in the tree.
I looked and saw...
A girl.
I heard her take three very deep breaths.
I asked, "Are you worried too?"

She nodded.
"I'm Brock."
"I'm Nelly."

"So why are *you* worried?"
"I just moved here. I don't know anyone."
"I'll sit with you," I said,
 and Nelly looked like she felt
 a little better.

I said, "I'll tell you about my friends.
Juan's funny. Jin's nice.
And Skitter makes the best costumes."
"I like yours," Nelly said.
"Thanks. I like yours too."

"You know," Nelly said, "I don't feel so worried up here."
"Yeah," I said. "But we can't stay up here forever."

I looked at Nelly.
I wanted her to meet my friends.
And I wanted to say happy birthday
to Juan and eat some cake!
So I asked, "Do you like cake, Nelly?"
Nelly nodded. "I love it!"

We were still worried,
but not like before.
It helped that we'd talked
about being worried.

I said, "Let's be brave."
"Like superheroes?" Nelly said.
I nodded. "Like superheroes."

"And we can always help each other if we feel more worried again. Right?"
"Right," I said.

I could feel my mind calming,
and my worry shrinking.

"On the count of three, let's swoop in," I told Nelly.
"Okay! 1, 2, 3..."

And we joined the party.
It was fun!

Best of all,
we weren't worried.